Sheila Tyrer Hughes' passion for reading developed naturally into a love of writing. After leaving school at 17, she worked as a trainee pathology lab technician before going to California in search of an adventure. There, she took care of children and horses before returning to Wales and becoming an English teacher. She loves mysteries, the countryside, ancient buildings and landscapes and losing herself in imaginary worlds. She is a mother and grandmother and lives in Cheshire. *The Red Shawl* is her fourth book for children.

The Red Shawl

Sheila Tyrer Hughes
Illustrations by Bee Buckmaster

AUSTIN MACAULEY PUBLISHERS™
LONDON • CAMBRIDGE • NEW YORK • SHARJAH

A CIP catalogue record for this title is available from the British Library.

ISBN 9781398461604 (Paperback)
ISBN 9781398461611 (ePub e-book)

www.austinmacauley.com

First Published 2023
Austin Macauley Publishers Ltd®
1 Canada Square
Canary Wharf
London
E14 5AA

For my granddaughters, Jessica and Eleanor.

Chapter 1
Another Garden,
Another Time

When Lily was a few months old, her mum, Kate, went back to work. Her father stayed at home. He carried out his business on a computer and enjoyed cooking – so there was always a meal ready when Lily's mum came home. All day long, Lily watched him and listened to him. Her eyes followed him everywhere, first from her cot, then from a quilted playpen.

Her first word was 'Da' for Daddy, then 'Mimi' instead of Mummy. Even Fiddler the cat became Fifi. The names stuck, somehow. It didn't matter. Lily was talking at last and her dad was over the moon. He read to her when he should have been working, made up stories while the dinner cooked, took her to the park and along country lanes whatever the weather. He let her feel the wind in her hair and the rain and snow on her face. He let her crumble soil between her fingers, feel the sand between her toes. He called her 'My little angel', 'My little star'.

Lily loved bright colours. She loved the flowers in the park and the hedgerows. She liked making patterns with pieces of coloured paper. She would cover a page with them and when she had finished, it would look like a riot of roses, a garden bursting with blooms. And that was exactly what it was meant to be.

"Whose garden is it?" her dad would ask.

"Lily's," she would answer, laughing. "It's Lily's garden."

"But Lily hasn't got a proper garden."

And that's what gave her dad the idea.

At the back of the house, they had a rather sad-looking lawn and a few sickly plants. The soil was thin and poor and Lily's dad had never been a gardener. He'd never had the time. At least, that was his excuse.

"Fancy having a beautiful lily and no garden for her to grow in," he said one day. "Shall we make a garden, Lily – a real garden with water and flower beds and trees – like the ones we've seen on the tele?"

Lily smiled and nodded excitedly. Then she gave her dad a great big hug.

First, a lorry came, with a load of good soil. Lily liked the smell of it. She put on her Wellington boots and watched the lorry tipping, burying the tired old garden beneath it. Her dad got some help. Two men came and made a winding path out of flat stones. They built a rockery at the bottom of the garden and made water trickle down into a pool. Then they brought new grass, rolled up like wallpaper.

"It's magic," said Lily as the bright, new lawn appeared. "Like Jack's beanstalk."

"Yes," said her dad, and he knew what she meant, for Jack's beanstalk had grown quickly, just like their new lawn – and 'Jack and the Beanstalk' was one of Lily's favourite stories.

When the men had finished, Lily's dad took her to a garden centre and together they chose the flowers they wanted for the garden. Lily liked flowers that were purple and white and blue and pink. She wanted lavender and thyme and lemon balm because they smelled so delicious. They filled the boot three times and had a wonderful time planting.

Lily had her own little fork and trowel and a soft pad for kneeling on. As they worked, she kept sniffing hugely, gulping the smells like delicious lemonade. She ran her finger along their leaves, some smooth and sharp, others rough and bubbly, enjoying the feel of them. Then she would stop to listen to the soft trickle of water over the stones. Her dad had never seen her so happy, so interested and involved.

When a robin landed on a discarded flowerpot, she froze like a statue and whispered to him. Then Lily's dad stopped working too. What was that noise? It wasn't the water, or the excited birds gathering in next door's lilac tree. No. It was Lily – and she was singing.

When Lily's mum came home, the planting was done.

Now all they could do was watch and wait for the flowers to grow and fill their spaces like the colours in Lily's pictures.

Lily was patient. She took her books outside and sat by the water. She chattered to the birds in a special way that she had, and sometimes she sang.

Frogs came to the pond.

Butterflies and bees visited the flowers.

A hedgehog found his way through the beeches and came in search of slugs and snails.

Her dad hung up food and more birds came: blue-tits and finches, blackbirds and doves.

"It's the best thing I ever did," said Lily's dad, and her mum agreed.

They tied a bell on to Fiddler's collar to warn the birds that he was around.

When Lily started school, she shared the garden with her new friend Megan and for four whole years, Lily's wonderful garden – and her best friend, Megan – were at the centre of her world.

Then something terrible happened, suddenly, like a clap of thunder from an empty sky. And when Lily had been told, it was as if the sun had gone out – or else the whole world had turned to grey like an old photograph.

Megan went away, suddenly, without a word or warning to her best friend.

It happened on a day in February, when Lily arrived at Sophie Miller's birthday party. Megan was supposed to be there too, but she didn't turn up. Sophie's mum tried telephoning but received no answer, so the party went ahead without her. It wasn't the same. Lily and Megan were like peas in a pod. Everyone said so. They liked the same books, the same games, and Megan loved to play in Lily's garden. She told Lily it was a magical place.

When Lily's dad came to collect her, he said a parcel had been delivered for her.

"Why?" said Lily. "It's not my birthday." Not for a moment did she think the parcel had anything to do with Megan. "Megan wasn't at the party," she said, frowning.

"Perhaps she was ill."

"But she would have phoned. We tell each other everything, you know we do."

"I'm sure there's a perfectly good explanation."

The parcel was the explanation. Inside it was a beautiful, old-fashioned, hand-knitted shawl. It was red, patterned with beautiful stitches and as soft as rabbit fur. There was a card with it in Megan's handwriting, much neater than Lily's. As she opened it, Lily felt her hand shaking.

Dear Lily,

I have to go and stay with my dad for a while.

He lives in Scotland. I couldn't tell you because I didn't know till today. I'll have to go to a different school. I'll miss you. My Scottish gran knitted this. I want you to have it. You can cuddle up in it when you watch tele. It will keep you warm and make you think of me. We can be pen-pals until I come home again.

Love from Megan xxx

Lily shivered. She folded the shawl into a triangle and put it around her shoulders. It felt wonderful and soft and made her think of her friend. Then she let her mum give her a great big hug. What would she do without Megan? Nothing would be fun anymore. The garden would lose its magic.

A month passed and Lily gave up watching for the postman. Megan had forgotten to give Lily her new address so Lily couldn't write to her. In all that time, she never once went into the garden. Then, one sunny spring morning, when Grandma had come over and was making some brownies, a noise made Lily jump. It was sudden and sharp, like the shattering of glass, and so unexpected that Lily's hand leapt in her lap and the red shawl slipped from her shoulders.

It was the barking of a dog – persistent, demanding. Lily stood up and walked to the French windows that opened into the garden. She turned the handle and opened the door. There it was again, calling to her, inviting her to go out into the garden. She moved carefully, like a wooden doll, down the steps and across the lawn.

"Is that you, Lily? Are you going into the garden?" Grandma called from the kitchen. But Lily didn't answer. The only voice she heard was that of a child calling from somewhere beyond the garden. It was a strange voice, not like someone from her school, no one she knew.

"Lupin. Fie on ye. If you do not be obedient, then you shall be cast out and no longer shall be my friend. Oh Lupin, do not run about so in Raphael's cabbages."

Lily walked slowly towards the sound, towards a strange wall at the end of the garden. Instead of the green gate there was a solid, wooden door there now. She'd never seen such a door – except on a castle – and *their* garden was bordered by a beech hedge, not a high wall. She lifted the iron ring. It was heavy and she needed two hands, but it turned easily and she pushed open the door.

****

Chapter 2
Effie and Lupin

Immediately, a little dog with a rough, brownish coat, the mixed colours of a marmalade cat, came tearing towards her. Lily lifted her hands to her face and drew herself in while the little dog ran a circle around her and dashed away again. When Lily looked through her fingers, she saw a girl standing by a row of cabbages, hands on hips and a determined expression on her thin little face. The girl was about her own age, but she wore a long, brown dress and an odd little hat.

The girl looked in her direction for a moment, then managed to grab the dog, just as an old man came into sight around the corner of a stone building. He was wheeling a wooden barrow, and his back and knees were bent.

"Good morrow to you, Master Raphael," said the girl. "I was just telling Lupin about your fine cabbages."

"And I will be telling Dame Euphemia to put that dog on the spit if I catch him scratting about in my cabbages again. 'Tis work enough to keep away the cattypillars."

The girl laughed. It was a merry sound, and the old man was smiling too as he lifted a hoe from the barrow and began to weed between the rows.

"Here, little wench," he said, "go tie up the tiresome creature and fill this pail wi' crawlers – if ye want any cabbages left for yer soup."

Then the old man straightened his back and touched his forehead with a wrinkled brown hand that looked like a tree root. Someone else had appeared – a lady in a long, grey habit.

Lily took a step towards them, but suddenly they were gone and she was walking back up her own garden path, on the other side of the wall.

"Ah, there you are," her grandma was saying. "I've brought you some juice and a chocolate biscuit. Don't stay out too long, will you? It's getting quite chilly." But Lily was just staring and frowning at the place where the door in the wall had been.

"Are you all right, dear?" her grandma was saying.

Lily turned and nodded. Then she smiled, really smiled, for the first time in weeks.

The next day, after school, it was raining. Lily sat by the French window, staring at the garden, listening intently for a little dog barking or the strange girl in the dull brown dress calling his name. Nothing! She must have imagined it, made it all up.

Her grandma watched her silence with a heavy heart. "I tell you what," she said, desperate to see Lily smile again, "I've done the ironing, and the dinner is in the oven. Let's go to the library. We can catch the bus into town and call at Raphael's for a drink and one of his delicious pastries."

Raphael! The name was like a spark in Lily's head. She stood up and began searching for her shoes. Raphael. Raphael. Raphael made pastries? But Raphael was a gardener with a crooked back and bent knees.

At the library, Lily's grandma pointed her in the direction of the junior fiction. "Go and have a look 'round," she said. "I'll come and help you find something when I've returned these."

Lily didn't reach the junior fiction. In the middle of the room was a stand filled with picture books, a mixture of new and old. Lily stopped.

Then a lady came over. She must be new. Lily hadn't seen her before.

"The local primary school is studying the Tudors. That's why we've put all these books together." She picked one up. "I love these picture books, don't you?"

Lily nodded.

"Are you doing the Tudors?" asked the lady. She didn't wait for a reply. "This is a nice one, full of wonderful pictures. You can really imagine what life must have been like."

Lily took the book from her and whispered a thank you, while the woman smiled kindly and went back to shelving her trolley of returned books. She found a corner and sat down on the floor. When she opened the book, somewhere in the middle, the first picture her eyes lighted on was of a monk in a long, brown habit, bending down by a row of vegetables. Beside him was a wooden wheelbarrow, just like the one the old man had been wheeling.

Lily snapped the book shut, sure that if she looked at another page, she would see old Raphael and the girl with the cheeky grin and the little dog, Lupin. She didn't look at any other books. The book about the Tudors was the only one Lily wanted. She held on to it tightly while her grandma chose two others to read to her. One of them was Grandma's own favourite, 'The Secret Garden'.

Lily had never been to Raphael's before. She was disappointed to see that there was no Raphael – no one who resembled the gardener she had seen. There were just girls in black trousers, white shirts and aprons. *Where's Raphael?* she wanted to ask, but she just sat quietly and nibbled at her pastry.

The next day, when Lily was eating her breakfast, she heard the little dog again. He was barking, yapping like mad. Lily suddenly thought, *He didn't bark at me like that. He just ran 'round me. He wanted me to play.*

She slipped from her chair and ran to the window.

"What is it, Lily? What's the matter?" her mother cried.

"It's Lupin," said Lily.

Her mother's eyes opened wide. First, she beamed, then she frowned. Her grandma shook her head and shrugged.

"Who's Lupin?"

But Lily had gone quickly from the window into the other room and was opening the door into the garden.

"You haven't finished your breakfast, Lily."

Before she had even stepped outside, Lily saw something come flying over the wall. She ran down the path to the wooden door. There were black and yellow caterpillars everywhere. She shook her head as more came flying over the wall and landed in her hair.

She lifted the heavy iron ring and opened the door. On the other side was the girl with the little dog yapping and jumping as she threw more caterpillars over the wall. Lily blinked at the strangeness of the scene and glanced back. Her own house faded before her eyes and when she had stepped through the door, it closed slowly behind her.

The girl stopped what she was doing and stared at Lily. "I can see thee today," she said. "I knew you were here, watching us. Lupin saw thee. Did you come because I crept into the chapel and did dip my fingers in the holy water and make a wish?"

Lily shook her head. "I don't think so. I came because your dog barked."

"Ah," said the girl, knowingly. "Verily, he is a clever creature, but oft times he is mischief itself and gets us both beaten." She smiled as if the memory of a beating was something amusing. Then she lifted the pail she was holding and peered deep inside it in a comical manner that made Lily laugh. When her brown face emerged, her eyes were crossed and there was a yellow-black caterpillar crawling across her nose.

Lily giggled. "What's your name?" she asked as the girl shook the caterpillar into her hand and threw it over the wall.

"Effie," she said. "What might yourn be?"

"Lily, Lily Masson. I live on the other side of the wall."

"Aye, I know," said Effie, "for when the ladies were at vespers once, I crept away from my chores and heard thee singing. I saw you working in your garden. But there were no sallets there and Raffy would think it a sin to grow no vegetables. I do not think it a sin. I am sure that God likes flowers as well as cabbages. I like the pool you have made, where the sparrows come to wash themselves."

"Did you ever come into the garden?"

"No. I was afeared. The gate was not always there. It is a different gate. There was no need to open it for I could see through the spaces in the wood. The ladies do not have such gates. They would not be strong enough. If the gate is not there, then I cannot see what is on the other side? I was afraid that if I was sorely tempted by the sin of curiosity, then the devil would take me and I might not return."

Lily gasped. She hadn't stopped to think that her own gate might disappear forever. She looked beyond Effie, to the grey stone building, long and low, and the gravel path that led through an arch to what appeared to be a courtyard. When she looked back at the wall, her own garden gate had reappeared.

"I must go," she said. "I have to go to school."

Effie frowned. "But will ye come back? Prithee, do come back. There are no other children here, though the ladies are kind enough."

"Where is your mother?"

"I have none."

"What about your father?"

"I have neither father nor mother, nor brother nor sister. My mother's life was taken when I was born and the ladies gave me shelter. I have only the ladies and Raffy and Lupin. And I will be beaten if they discover I have dipped my dirty fingers in the holy water and wished for something more because I am ungrateful."

"I'll come back – if I can," said Lily. "I promise." Then she ran towards the familiar gate and the world behind her disappeared.

****

Chapter 3
Hide and Seek
in The Dairy

Lily's mum and dad and grandma could see a change in Lily. They were relieved – and puzzled at the same time, for though she smiled more and responded to their words with a nod or a shake of the head, she had said very little since Megan had gone. The thing was, Lily's head was full of Effie and Lupin and the strange world beyond the wall. But unless she heard their voices, she did not step into the garden. She was afraid that if she went through her own garden gate and the other world wasn't there, she would somehow break the spell and never see them again.

"Who's Lupin?" her mum asked again, gently, when they were eating one of grandma's pies.

Lily slipped from her chair and went to look through the window, listening intently.

"Is he a... new friend?"

Lily nodded slowly. How could she tell them about Effie and Lupin? Who would believe her? She finished her meal and went to study her book.

"At least she's showing interest in something again," said Kate. "I just wish she'd talk to me."

"She will," said her grandma, "when she's ready."

"Does she talk to you, say anything at all?"

Grandma shook her head. "She really misses Megan."

"Perhaps we ought to go away for a while, have a holiday," said Kate. "I'll think about it."

"Peter won't agree, not with that new contract."

"Then we shall have to go without him. He won't mind, if it cheers Lily up."

Suddenly, Lily was at her side, pointing at a word in her book.

"Cistercian. The Cistercian order of monks and nuns."

Lily looked up at her mum, waiting for more.

Kate turned a page. "They lived in abbeys and priories and spent their time praying and taking care of the sick." Her eyes lit up. "The Cistercians were also good gardeners, I believe. Wait a minute. It says here that they believed in a simple life of hard work and worship, but people gave them gifts anyway, and they became wealthy against their will. They grew vegetables and herbs and fruit trees – and it sounds as if they did bed and breakfast as well if any traveller came through. They sound rather nice, don't they?"

Lily nodded, but her words were stuck somewhere. Then Lupin barked, and she was aware of another world – a world without an empty space where her best friend should be, a strange and exciting world she could step into, like Dorothy in *The Wizard of Oz.*

Suddenly, there was a ripple of laughter and Lily glanced up to see if Kate and her grandma had heard, but Kate was staring into space and Grandma was listening to the radio and busy with some sewing. They both looked at Lily and smiled when they saw her slide open the French windows and step into the garden.

Lily didn't hesitate. She almost ran down the path, turned the ring that lifted the iron latch and stepped into the priory garden, for that, she decided, was what it was. The lady she had glimpsed on her last visit had been wearing a dull, grey habit, just like the nun in the book.

As soon as the door closed in the high stone wall, she spotted Lupin, barking excitedly and bouncing like a rubber ball at the foot of an apple tree. From its branches, two skinny legs dangled down and Lily knew they were Effie's. Suddenly, Effie dropped like a cat and rolled over in the grass, shrieking when Lupin dived at her and began licking her face.

Lily laughed.

If only her mother could have seen her.

Effie heard her and leapt to her feet. "Lily, you came back. You came back to see us. Look. Lupin! 'Tis Lily."

Then Lupin ran towards her and bounced and licked.

"You're just like Tigger," said Lily, "full of bounce."

"Who is Tigger? Is he a dog?"

"No, he's a tiger in a story."

Effie's eyes lit up. "Ah. Dame Euphemia doth tell me stories sometimes about the saints and about the kings and queens. But I have never heard a story about a tiger. What is a tiger?"

"It's a cat, a big cat with black and yellow stripes. I'll show you next time I come," said Lily. "I shall draw one for you or else find a picture in a book."

"A book?" said Effie in astonishment. "You do have a book of your own? But you are only a child like me. I have never touched a book. If I am very good and no one has any complaint of me, the ladies unwrap the linen and let me see their books. Methinks they are gifts from God for I have never seen anything so beautiful. They are bound in leather and bright stones. But I like the pictures best. They are as bright as the stars and the flowers in the meadow."

"What are they about?"

"I cannot tell for I cannot read. And even if I could, it is a strange script and not the words we speak, though I know a little of it for I have learned it from the ladies when they say their prayers."

Effie dropped to her knees and bowed her head.

"*Pater noster qui es in caelis, sanctificetur nomen tuum...* Our Father, who art in Heaven..."

But Lupin was having none of it. It was quite clear he wanted to play. Effie laughed and jumped to her feet. "Come, Lily," she said. "Let us play hide and go seek. I shall hide for I knoweth all the best places and Lupin will seek me out and show you where I am. Dost thou know 'The Rattling Bog'? 'Tis a song that Raffy teaches me when the ladies are at their prayers. Two choruses of it will give me time to conceal myself." And she started to sing.

> "Hey-ho the rattling bog,
> The bog down in the valley-oh,
> A rare bog, a rattling bog..."

"No," said Lily, laughing, "but I can sing 'Ragtime Cowboy Joe'. My dad taught it to me – and Megan and I used to sing it together."

Effie picked up the squirming little dog and handed him to Lily. Then away she ran, barefooted, like a hare across the grass, ignoring the gravel, skirting the vegetable plot and disappearing through an archway into the small, cloistered courtyard.

Lily's heart was pounding. What if someone else saw her? What if they caught her and locked her up because they thought she was a thief? She began to sing.

"He always sings raggy music to the cattle
as he swings back and forward in the saddle
on a horse that is syncopated-gaited.
What a funny metre to the roar of his repeater.

How they run when they..." Lily stopped when she saw Raphael trundling around the corner with his wheelbarrow. She waited, frozen to the spot, wondering if she should speak to him, or if her voice would startle him. The little dog lay quietly in her arms and she rubbed his soft ears. There was no way to follow Effie but past the gardener. She took a deep breath and began walking.

Raphael was whistling softly to himself. Then he took off his soft hat and scratched his head. Lily was astonished to see so much hair beneath it. As she walked towards him, he never once looked up, but concentrated on hoeing and picking up weeds. She tiptoed past him, Lupin still in her arms. Just as she was passing through the archway, a voice behind her said, "Good day to ye, young mistress. I think ye'll find she's hiding in the dairy. She has a liking for cheese, has young Effie."

Lily gasped and smiled. She put Lupin down and ran after him across the cobbled yard. They wove through the empty cloisters, just for the fun of it, tore down a passage, through a doorway into another smaller yard and found themselves in a cold room where there was a strong, sour smell. Cheese. Lupin yapped excitedly and disappeared behind some pails and barrels. A squeal of laughter told Lily that she had found her friend and when Effie crawled out, she was licking her fingers and wiping her mouth. Raphael was right.

Suddenly, the room was darker. When Lily turned, she saw a tall figure in the doorway, arms folded. The figure didn't speak, but she was angry – or pretending to be – Lily couldn't tell.

Lily stepped back against the wall, hoping the lady wouldn't see her – but there was something hanging there, spoons and stirrers and paddles for making the butter and cheese. They rattled and clattered against each other. The lady turned. But then, some wooden pails clattered to the floor, deliberately overturned by Effie, and the lady strode forward. She grabbed Lupin roughly by the scruff of his neck and Effie by the woven belt that was tied around her shift. She lifted them both, Lupin whining and Effie still snorting with laughter, and carried them from the dairy like two bags of carrots.

Lily couldn't move, yet, at the same time, she was tingling with excitement. She giggled, picturing Effie's laughing face. The sound echoed strangely. She and Megan had giggled a lot – once, a long time ago, it seemed. It felt good, but then Lily wondered what punishment Effie would have to suffer. Would she be beaten again? Should Lily wait?

She picked up the fallen pails and stood on tiptoe to look into an enormous tub. It was full of something thick and creamy. She glanced towards the doorway before reaching up and dipping in one finger. She liked cheese, too – and this was delicious. Then she heard footsteps and ran back the way she had come, across the cobbled yard, through the arch and over the gravel that seemed to crunch so loudly under her feet she was sure someone would hear her. Raphael was still busy among the turnips and carrots. He smiled as she flitted past him.

"Fare thee well, young mistress," he said softly as she slipped back through her own garden gate.

****

Chapter 4
Effie's Gift and
A Tiger Wish

Lily remembered what Effie had said about her garden, about the birds and the water and the flowers. Next day, she went out to the garden shed, collected some tools and began weeding. Dad had been so busy lately, she hardly saw him. He certainly had no time to tidy the flower beds. They were a mess, and suddenly Lily felt ashamed. Her dad had made this garden for her, and she had neglected it. As she knelt, forking the soil and filling a bucket with weeds, she thought about Megan and tears slipped silently down her cheeks. She shivered and got up, but before she had taken a step towards the house her grandma was beside her and the lovely red shawl was wrapped around her shoulders and tied behind her back. Her grandma didn't speak, but walked quietly back to the house.

"At least she's doing something again," said Kate when Grandma stood beside her. "I'm so worried about her, Mum."

"No need," said Grandma. "I'm not sure what's happening, but she's working through it is our Lily. Just give her time."

In the garden, amongst the weeds, Lily had made a discovery. A tiny flower, a blue star with a white centre, was reaching for the sun. She cleared around it, whispering encouragement. Then she remembered. One day last autumn, when she and her mum had been out shopping, they came back to find her dad had been busy. He'd been planting 'secrets' he said, surprises for Lily. This tiny blue star must be one of them. Lily hugged the shawl around her, wondering how many more she would find. If she didn't take care of the flower beds, they would be choked and lost. She couldn't bear that. And so, she worked a little every day, finding more blue stars and tiny daffodils, pale pink hyacinths and the pointy leaves of irises.

Sometimes, while she worked, she heard the distant bark of Lupin or the excited squeal of Effie. Once, she heard Raphael's gruff voice scolding, but always, it seemed, there was a chuckle in his voice. Sometimes, she dared to peer through her own gate, beyond the high hedge that bordered their garden, but there was nothing on the other side except meandering paths of badger and fox through a wide stretch of common land, some tangled bushes – and a copse of tall old trees where rooks built their twiggy nests.

Once or twice a week, Lily saw the solid wooden door with the iron ring – and then she slipped away to visit Effie.

Always, Effie was overjoyed to see her. And when she had finished her chores, sweeping floors and strewing them with fresh rushes, cleaning square wooden trenchers (plates) with sand and water and scratchy twigs and removing stones and caterpillars from the garden, Effie would take Lily to another part of the priory. They watched the butter being churned in the dairy and wine being made in the buttery. They followed the smell of baking bread to the pastry, the hot, steamy room where great loaves and meat pies were being made by over-dressed ladies with red scrubbed arms and sweating faces.

And always, the ladies scolded kindly and sent Effie on her way with the threat of more work for her – and a taste of whatever was being made. A crust of coarse brown bread that Effie and Lily had to toss between them until it was cool enough to eat. A spoonful of curd from the cheese making – and even a small wooden cup, brimming with purple wine that Lily pulled a face at and Effie swallowed in a gulp. One day, Effie took Lily into the chapel and they stood on tiptoes, their hands on the lip of the font, looking at their reflections in the holy water.

"Where's your room, Effie?" Lily asked one day. "Where do you sleep?"

Effie showed her, proudly it seemed. Up a stone staircase they scampered and down a narrow passageway. Halfway along was a small recess with a tiny window, nothing more than a vantage point where one could enjoy the view of the countryside, or look out for visitors approaching – or enemies. Tucked into it, filling its width was what seemed to Lily nothing more than a bag of straw. Effie leapt on to it, tossing and wriggling until it was like a nest. There was little else, just the stone floor, a straw mattress and a thin, grey blanket. Lily was speechless. She thought of her own room with its comfortable bed and lavender duvet, of the carpet and the pictures and the cupboards full of clothes and toys and books. There was no way she could tell Effie about all that. Then she laughed. Effie was curled up like a mouse, her thumb in her mouth, and she was snoring, or pretending to. She opened one eye and squinted up at Lily, a giggle escaping among the snores. Then she leapt to her feet.

"Lily," she said, seriously now. "I knoweth what the ladies tell me is right, that I should thank God for all His goodness and not ask for that which He has not chosen to give me..." – she touched Lily's soft cotton sweatshirt with her fingertips – "but verily, I would dearly like to see a creature with stripes... and hold a book as if it were my very own."

Always, Lily came on the spur of the moment, when she heard Lupin or Effie or both and saw the heavy, wooden door. Afraid that they would disappear if she hesitated, she never took the time to go into the house and find a present for Effie.

"Oh, Effie!" she said. "I'm not a very good friend, am I? I promised you a picture and I keep forgetting to bring one. Next time, I shall bring a picture and a book for you to see."

"And I will give you a gift." Effie dropped to her knees and burrowed beneath the straw mattress. When she stood up again, she was holding a bunch of tiny dried flowers – herbs and leaves that Lily could smell. "'Twill keep the devil away," explained Effie.

"Thank you," said Lily, and she gave her new friend a hug.

Suddenly, from somewhere below, a voice was calling. There was an urgency about it and when Lily looked at Effie, she saw something in her face that she had never seen before. Effie was afraid.

"Effie! Come hither, girl. This is no time to be playing tricks. There's work to be done, and extra chores for thee."

It wasn't a cruel voice, or even an unkind one, but there was a note to it that gave Lily a shiver of fear. They ran back along the passage and skidded to a halt, for a nun had appeared at the foot of the stairs. The light was behind her, so Lily could not see the expression on her face, but she heard a tremor in her voice.

"Come back soon, Lily," said Effie, "for there is evil in the land and I fear that soon we will all be driven away. Our king bears no love for places such as this and we may not be allowed to live here much longer. Dame Johanna has called a gathering to discuss what is to be done. I have to help make ready."

Then she was gone, skipping down the cold steps in her bare feet.

Back in her own living room, Lily opened the library book and found a picture of Henry the Eighth, whose hatred of the Catholic Church drove him to wipe out the monasteries and drive away the monks and nuns who lived there. He stole their gold and silver and returned their land to his loyal subjects.

Upstairs, Lily's grandma was changing beds. She lifted Lily's pillows and frowned as she picked up a tiny bunch of dried herbs. She held them to her nose but couldn't identify the smells. When she had made the bed, she returned the posy.

"What's that under your pillow, Lily? Is it a good luck charm?" she asked when Lily came upstairs with her book.

Lily stared at her and nodded.

"Did you make it?"

Lily shook her head.

"Then who did?"

"Effie."

"Who's Effie? Another new friend?"

Lily nodded her head slowly and stared at her grandma. She wanted to tell her but the words would not come. Then she closed her book and went in search of *Winnie the Pooh* – and a picture of a real tiger. She'd seen one in a magazine Grandma had bought. It was just a car advertisement or something, but it was a good picture.

When she had cut it out, she wrapped picture and book in a plastic bag and hid them at the bottom of the garden so that whenever she saw the door in the wall, she could take them to Effie.

The next afternoon felt hot and sticky, though Grandma said it was too early in the year for thunderstorms. Yet there was that tingling feeling in the yellow air and a silence in the sky as if everything were waiting.

Lily, too, felt tingly inside, nervous and scared. Something was wrong. She just knew it. She liked the feeling of the red shawl so she tied it around her and went into the garden. What if something had already happened to Effie? What if she wasn't there? Lily felt she couldn't bear it if she lost Effie too without saying goodbye. She sat on the garden seat and almost immediately she heard noises coming from the other side of the hedge. But they were not the sounds she was used to and the door in the wall had not appeared. Instead, the beech hedge had become hawthorn and there was something appearing that looked like a farm gate. She got up, slowly, listening to men's voices and the clattering of hooves. Then she picked up the plastic bag from its hiding place, pulled back the bar and slipped cautiously through. Everything was different. Where the priory had stood there was now a farm with sheds and barns and haystacks – and she was standing at the edge of a potato patch. She could hear sheep bleating and hens clucking, and in an open building where the archway had been, a man in a leather apron was holding up the hoof of the biggest horse that Lily had ever seen.

****

Chapter 5
Lady Isabella Dawe

Lily stood still for a moment, puzzled and alarmed. It was just as if she had turned over the wrong page in a history book. She was in a different time. But she hadn't finished with the last time. She had to know what happened to Effie. She needed to keep her promise about the picture and the book. She squeezed her eyes shut and held the book tightly as she thought about Effie and willed her to be there. The unfamiliar sounds grew faint, but when she opened her eyes, there was no Effie or Lupin, just that same tingling in the air and the sound of a horse's hooves in the familiar cobbled courtyard.

Lily ran around Raphael's garden and stood in the shadows of the wall, peeping through. A man was dismounting from a tired horse. Raphael, with a piece of old sacking over his back, was holding the horse's head, stroking its nose. The rider was soaked. He removed his hat and shook the water from it, then he hammered on the first door he saw, not caring, it seemed, if the nuns were at their prayers.

W"Dame Johanna! Dame Johanna!" he shouted impatiently. "In the name of Heaven, you must make ready! Dame Johanna!"

Lily was astonished when the door opened and Effie stood there.

"Fie on ye, sir," she said, in a bold voice. "'Tis four of the clock. The ladies are at vespers and would not be disturbed unless the refectory was afire."

"Aroint, child! 'Tis no time for jesting," yelled the man. Then he lowered his voice. "A lady is come from the court of King Henry and needs the protection of these walls and the good dames within. She is from these parts and as a child was known to Dame Johanna. For God's sake, find your mistress and give me some wine and a bite to eat for my legs feel like hollow reeds and my stomach is as empty as a beggar's purse."

At that moment, the storm arrived, and bullets of rain beat down on the cobbles. Effie bid the man enter while Raphael led his horse to a warm stable, and just as Effie was pushing the door to, lightning flashed, illuminating the red tiles of the roofs and the tiny face of someone hiding beneath the arch.

Effie waved frantically and called to Lily. "Prithee, wait anon." She put her hand on her heart and pushed the door to.

Lily melted into the shadows while the thunder and lightning battled in the sky above her. It seemed forever, as if in this moment, sheltering beneath the arch of an old priory, touching the cold stones and smelling the unfamiliar smells of another century, the storm had stopped the clock and nothing would ever change again.

But the storm moved on as storms always do. A break in the clouds shone with silver light, the cobbles steamed and Lily was aware of a bell clanging away to her left on the outer wall.

Raphael appeared, shuffling from the stable to open the main gate – as he had for the stranger – after peering through a small door in the wall. A horse came through without spirit or urgency and when Raphael closed the gate, its rider slid to the ground and leaned heavily against the saddle before collapsing to his knees on the cobbles.

It's just a boy, thought Lily. He doesn't look much older than me. Then Effie appeared, running towards Raphael and the visitor. And behind her, walking quickly was one of the dames.

Suddenly, the rain stopped completely and the split in the clouds grew bigger. As Lily watched, the exhausted traveller threw back his hood...

"It's a girl!" Lily gasped, and instinctively, without thinking of the consequences, she ran to help.

Between them, Dame Euphemia (after whom Effie was named) and Effie raised the girl to her feet. Her braided hair fell heavily about her shoulders, and through exhausted tears she managed to smile her gratitude at them. Dame Euphemia untied the wet cloak and draped it over the saddle.

"Take good care of the noble beast, Master Raphael," she said quietly. "It has carried Lady Isabella Dawe a very long way, has it not, Isabella?"

The girl's face was deathly pale.

"*Psst!* Effie, give her this!"

Without another thought, Lily had taken the red shawl from around her shoulders and was pushing it at Effie. Effie wrapped the warm soft wool around the shivering girl, and the girl looked up, straight into Lily's eyes. "Grammercy," she whispered. Thank you.

What a lovely word, thought Lily – and she smiled back.

But Dame Euphemia, who hadn't seen Lily, exclaimed to Effie, "Where in the name of the Saints did you get such a thing, a wisp of a girl like you? Did you steal it?"

"Nay. Thee knows better than to ask it. Tis thyself taught me right from wrong and what shall happen if I break God's laws."

"Aye, well, young miss, we shall speak of it later. For now, it appears a wonderful thing and has brought warmth to our visitor's cheeks." She touched the shawl. "But verily, I say I have never touched anything so soft – and such a colour."

They moved slowly across the yard. Then more nuns appeared and the young Lady Isabella was ushered into the priory amid worried looks and whispers.

Effie dodged through them and beckoned Lily to follow her. They ran to the stable where Raphael was rubbing down the weary horse with straw. They stood in the doorway and watched as he murmured softly to the tired animal, its head in a bucket of mash.

"Who is Lady Isabella, Raffy, and wherefore has she come here?"

"D'ye think 'tis any of thy business, young wench? Mayhap 'tis better tha knows nowt about it. Methinks tha'll know soon enow. Aye. We all will." He turned back to the horse then faced them again, looking directly at Lily. "And as fer the young mistress here, I know not from whence she hails, but I do know 'tis better she leave this place. 'Tis not safe, and I know not what shall become of us all."

"But who is she, Raff?"

Raphael sighed. He knew Effie would not give up until she was satisfied. He left off rubbing down the horse and leaned against the wooden partition that divided the stalls.

"She be the first child of Sir Robin Dawe. She has been at the court of... *his royal majesty.*" He said the last words as if they left a sour taste in his mouth, and when he spat into the straw Effie gasped at the insult to their king. "She was lady-in-waiting to his erstwhile queen. As to why she should leave in sich a hurry and under cover of night, I know not, though even a lummock sich as I can guess – for his royal majesty has a liking for a pretty face."

"Perhaps she has come to warn you?" whispered Lily. "Because the king is destroying all the monasteries and priories."

Effie shook her head, frowning at Lily. "But that cannot be true. They are places of God. His work is done here. The ladies are kind. They take care of the sick. They took care of me. Wherefore does the king want to destroy our home?"

Raphael shook his head slowly. "Tha must ask the dames," he said sadly, "for I am but a lowly servant and have no place in the concerns of a king."

"Come, Lily," said Effie, in a small voice that didn't sound like hers.

Then she took a deep breath, flung out her arm and proclaimed dramatically, "Thee must be gone, away from this place. For we are doomed. Thee must away to the market place and tell all who will heed that we fought bravely to the end and died to save these walls." Then she put her hand to her heart and fell to her knees.

Lily laughed and pulled Effie to her feet and they both giggled.

They ran to the garden, to a quiet corner of the orchard, and there Lily took out the book at last and gave it to Effie.

Effie's mouth fell open – and stayed open as she stared and stared at it, running her finger over the cover, tracing the picture. Then she sucked her breath in and closed her mouth. But she couldn't find any words.

"Open it," said Lily.

Slowly, Effie lifted the cover and saw the words and pictures. Winnie-the-Pooh and a honey-pot. Winnie-the-Pooh and bouncing Tigger. Then, she began turning the pages quickly, laughing like a brook.

"Shall I read it to you?" asked Lily.

Effie gaped at her and nodded.

"Winnie the Pooh woke up suddenly in the middle of the night and listened..."

When a voice called, they drew themselves into the shadows of the trees and the high walls, for Effie would not move until the story was finished.

Even then, she just sat and stared at the book as if it was the most miraculous thing she had ever seen. She touched it lovingly with her grubby fingertips and when she looked up at Lily, her eyes glistened with tears. Then she found a picture of gloomy Eeyore and said he looked just like Raphael when his back was a-troubling him.

Lily put her arms around Effie and they held each other tightly until they heard Lupin barking excitedly and were aware of movement, and hustle and bustle in the courtyard.

"I wish I could stay," said Lily, but she knew she could not. "I wish I could leave you the book," she said, "but I know it doesn't belong here."

She took out the magazine picture and handed it to Effie. "Here's a picture of a real tiger," she said.

Effie touched her head and her heart and sucked in a great noisy breath. "Verily, are there really such beasts?"

Lily closed her eyes for a moment. Yes, she wanted to say. There are tigers and camels and elephants and giraffes. And that's a photograph, not a painting. That's why it is so smooth and you cannot feel the paint. For she could tell what Effie was thinking as she ran her fingers over the page.

Then Lupin barked, frantically, it seemed, and Effie leapt to her feet.

"I must away and attend to Lupin. Will ye return soon, Lily? For if too many nights pass, ye may not find me here."

"I'll try," said Lily. "I really will."

Effie glanced anxiously towards the courtyard and was gone, clutching the picture tightly in her hand.

"Take care," whispered Lily.

****

Chapter 6
"Fare Thee Well, Lily"

The next day, Lily's world was shaken again.

"We're going away for a week, Lily," said Kate.

Lily's eyes opened wide in horror. She looked towards the window, out at the garden. Her heart was pounding. Her two worlds were colliding, crashing into each other. "But we can't," she said.

Her mum closed her eyes for a moment and breathed slowly. *Lily was talking.*

She mustn't say the wrong thing. She felt as though she were treading on egg-shells.

"Why, Lily?" she said gently. "Why can't we go? I thought a change would do us all good. We'll go somewhere we've never been before, somewhere new and exciting."

"But I can't leave Effie. I promised."

Her mum thought quickly. *Effie isn't real!*

"She could come with us."

Lily shook her head. "She won't leave Lupin. She's afraid to come through the gate."

"Who's Lupin?"

The words that came out were like an avalanche.

"A dog, a lovely little brown dog. He's all she's got. She doesn't have a mum or a dad or a book of her own, or any toys. She doesn't even have a proper bed – and sometimes they beat her, but she doesn't seem to mind that – and now the king is going to destroy her home and she doesn't know what's going to happen."

And suddenly, Lily started to cry – not noisily, with hiccups and jerking sobs but quietly with shaking hands and little shudders. She looked around for the comfort of Megan's red shawl and instead found the warmth of her mum's arms around her.

"Do you want this, Lily?" It was Grandma in the doorway. She was holding the red shawl. "It was on the hedge," she explained. "You must have left it there yesterday when you were in the garden. But we shall have to dry it first."

Lily pressed the damp shawl to her cheek. "I gave it to Lady Isabella," she said. "She was so wet after her ride from London. She thanked me. She said 'Grammercy'. Isn't it a lovely word? I shall always remember it."

"Do you want to tell me about them, Lily?"

Lily nodded.

When the shawl was dry, Lily hugged it to her and sat near the window, making a list of everyone and everything she had seen. No matter if some of the words were spelt wrongly, she had to remember every single thing. Everything she smelt and touched and saw.

Then something from the garden suddenly drew her attention away from her book. She jumped up and went to the window. Kate watched; her grandma watched – as Lily slid open the doors and went out.

Kate followed her, carrying the red shawl. There was a nip in the air. She slipped it around Lily's shoulders and stood on the step as Lily walked down the garden. What was she looking at? What had she seen?

At first, Lily had heard the now-familiar sound of horses' hooves on cobble stones. But there were voices, too – men's voices, someone shouting, giving orders, laughing – and in amongst it all, Lupin's frantic barking.

By the time Lily reached the bottom of the garden, the noises had ceased, and what she saw made her gasp. A figure was standing by the gate in the hedge. A small grey figure, wrapped in a bonnet and cloak. It was Effie, and squirming in her arms was Lupin.

"You came to me," said Lily. "Weren't you afraid?"

"Sorely," said Effie. "But seven nights have passed and ye did not return."

"I heard horses – and men," said Lily. "I was just on my way. I can't come if the door isn't there."

Effie was staring over Lily's shoulder. "Is that your home?"

Lily nodded.

"And the beautiful lady in the strange clothes – is she your mother?"

"Yes."

"And your father? Where is he? Does he fight for the king? He must be very rich."

"My father is working," said Lily. "He's always busy... But I have a grandmother who visits us all the time."

Effie touched her arm. "Then verily, ye are blessed, and I am glad that Lupin made me brave enough to step through your gate."

"You've come to say goodbye, haven't you?"

Effie nodded. "They are taking away the stones of our house. They have already burnt the books and were filled with mirth as they did so – while the ladies and I wept."

"Where will you go, Effie? What will you do?"

"Ye remember the Lady Isabella, who came in great haste from the court of the king some weeks past? She is betrothed to a young man and will soon be wed. She has vowed that she will teach me how to be a lady's maid. For she sayeth I have an uncommon curiosity and quick tongue, which must, forsooth, come from a noble father, though I know him not."

51

"What about Lupin?"

"She has a liking for Lupin, and he can live in the stables."

"And Raphael? He's too old to get another job."

"'Tis true. Raffy has nigh on two score years. But the Lady Isabella would not see him cast out without a home or friend. He is to be gardener at her new home, for the Lady Isabella has seen the gardens of a king and wishes to grow flowers – as well as sallets. She must grow sallets, for without his onions and cabbages I believe Raffy would be as sour as an unripe plum."

They laughed.

"And the ladies? Where will they go? They are not harmed, are they?"

"Nay, 'tis only their feelings and hearts are wounded. They will return to their families and be as they were."

"Oh, Effie, I'm so glad you have somewhere nice to live."

Effie turned to go. "Ours was but a small house with only two and twenty ladies. When the soldiers had burnt the books, they did not look further than the chapel. They took the silver from the altar and did not expect that the ladies had more. For Dame Johanna was not accustomed to wear fine clothes and jewellery as some do." Here, Effie looked around her. "Before the soldiers came, Raffy dug a deep hole in the middle of the cabbage patch and there the ladies buried everything they did not want the king to find." She grinned. "No one would look in a cabbage patch."

"Effie! Make haste before Lady Isabella changes her mind." It was Dame Euphemia. "Effie! Where are you, child? Come, say farewell now, while yet there is time."

"I must be gone." Effie screwed up her face in a comical fashion as Lily had seen her do when tears were not far away. "Fare thee well, Lily. I will remember thee always and thy book and garden of flowers. I will remember how thee smells and how different thy garments feel. And I will bless the angels who sent thee to be a friend to Effie."

Lily threw her arms around Effie and poor Lupin yelped as he was squashed between them.

"Do you still have the picture?"

"Alas, no. Dame Euphemia found it beneath my bed and threw it on the fire. She said it was the work of the devil and crossed herself three times and cleansed her hands in the holy water."

"Effie! Come hither at once. This is no time for games. Lady Isabella is leaving."

"Fare thee well, Lily."

Effie turned and was gone.

And, without thinking, Lily ran after her.

From the house Kate and Grandma saw Lily standing, staring at the garden gate.

"Effie, stop!"

They touched hands one last time and Lily didn't hesitate, though she felt a great lump in her throat. She took the red shawl from around her shoulders and thrust it at Effie. "Hide it under your cloak," she said. "When you are cold, it will keep you warm and when you are lonely, think of me and know that I will be thinking of you – wherever you are – always."

She stroked Lupin's soft ears and turned away, back to her own time, her own world, where her family was waiting.

****

Chapter 7
Buried Treasure

A few days later, Lily and Kate and Grandma were sitting before a roaring log fire in a tiny fisherman's cottage at the edge of the sea. It had been too cold for bathing or sitting about on the beach so they had hired bicycles – all three of them – and had pedalled happily through quiet country lanes and down woodland paths. They wore warm jumpers and stopped in magical places for picnics and in the evenings, they sat before a fire, listening to the waves rushing over rocks. Slowly, in her own time, Lily told Kate and Grandma about Effie and Lupin and Raphael – and what had happened to her red shawl.

"You gave it away?" Kate said quietly. "But Megan... I thought..."

Grandma put a finger to her lips.

"She needed it more," said Lily. "She has no mum or dad, no brother or sister, no real family at all. She has no toys or books or nice clothes – but she was always laughing."

"She was there when you needed her," said Grandma.

"That's what Effie said about me," said Lily.

"Then you helped each other."

Kate gave her a big hug and Grandma went to make them all a cup of creamy hot chocolate.

"Right!" she said, when they were all curled up on the sofa. "I vote we go to the Lost Gardens of Heligan tomorrow. I think you'll like it there, Lily."

Lily was entranced. She loved the giant trees, the secret corners and magical wild places. Instead of wishing at the wishing well, she said thank you – for Effie and Lupin and the amazing things she had seen.

By the time they got home, two things had happened. One, their neighbour, Mrs Jellicoe, had decided to go and live with her widowed sister. She was selling her house privately to her cousin's daughter. And two, Mrs Jellicoe told them that there was a proposed small development of houses on a part of the common.

Kate explained to Lily. They agreed. They couldn't let it happen.

"It's common land," said Kate to Grandma. "It belongs to everyone, doesn't it? Surely, they can't be allowed to build on it."

"Who knows?" said Grandma. "People don't graze their sheep or cattle there anymore. It's just a piece of waste ground as far as THEY are concerned. And they need more houses. It's as simple as that."

Lily and Kate went upstairs and looked out over the common.

"Do you know exactly where the priory was, Lily?"

"I think so."

"Then we have to tell them – if they don't already know. There are usually records about such places."

"It was only a small priory – not a big important one."

"Let's look, shall we?"

It felt strange, walking through the tangled grass, avoiding the brambles where Raphael's cabbage rows had been so carefully tended.

"The arch was there," Lily pointed out, "and the cobbled yard, and the house. And over there was the main gate. That's where the Lady Isabella came through and I gave her my shawl."

"Ah, was that when Grandma found it on the hedge?"

"Effie must have put it there. Dame Euphemia thought she'd stolen it."

Beneath the copse of tall old trees, the ground was lumpy, hard. They scraped around a bit but too many years had passed and too many leaves had fallen. If indeed there were any stones left, they were buried deep.

"The foundations will be here, even if the stones were plundered," said Kate.

"There was a farm here afterwards, but that's gone, too."

Kate didn't ask. It was hard enough accepting what Lily said about Effie and the priory. She and Grandma had seen Lily in the garden. Not once had they seen her leave it.

"We need evidence," Kate said.

Then Lily remembered that Raphael had buried things in the cabbage patch where no one would think to look.

"Raphael dug a big hole," she said. "He used an axe for digging, for he hadn't a spade like ours." She gasped then, suddenly remembering. "And they buried stuff in the garden because they didn't want the king to get it."

"But they would come back for it, surely."

Lily shrugged. "Perhaps they weren't able to."

"Come on, Lily, it's worth a try. Your dad knows someone who's got a metal detector. We'll give him a ring."

Lily walked carefully from the garden gate, working out the distance, picturing Raphael and his wheelbarrow. They made flags out of dusters and she marked the four corners of the vegetable patch. To and fro, Sean went with his metal detector while Lily and Kate watched, fingers crossed. Suddenly, there was a high-pitched beeping. The machine was fairly jumping in Sean's hands.

The grass was clumpy, the turf thick. It took some hard work to clear it before they could start digging. Sean picked up the spade, but Kate held his arm.

"No. We can't do this. It has to be done properly. We might do more harm than good. I wish I knew a good archaeologist, one we can trust with Lily's secret."

"In case I'm wrong, you mean," said Lily, "and they don't find anything."

Sean smiled at them both. "Funny you should say that, Kate. I just happen to know a good chap, local, working over at Pennycroft Farm where they're excavating a Roman tile factory. He's a bit older than me, went to school with my brother. I'll give him a ring."

And that was only the beginning.

The archaeologist came over. His name was Simon Green and they all liked him immediately. He was just one of those people you felt you had always known. Kate persuaded Lily to tell him her story. He listened quietly until she had finished and, for a few moments, didn't say a word.

"You don't believe me, do you?"

Simon Green took Lily's hand. "On the contrary," he said. "Though it's a strange story, I have heard stranger – and I do believe it, every word. I was convinced there had been an abbey or priory somewhere hereabouts, but I could find no real record of it."

"Then why did you...?"

"Old maps, names – look, I'll show you."

From his rucksack he drew out some laminated photocopies of maps and photographs and spread them out on the table. "See, here's one clue. Did you know that before your house was built, there was a lane here called Applegarth? That's an old orchard. And look at these uneven mounds. Perhaps they were fishponds – or other buildings. In the seventeen hundreds, there was a farm here called The Grange. It was destroyed in a fire in 1806. Grange farms were associated with monasteries."

"If there are so many clues, then why has no one dug here before?"

"Search me; it's a mystery. Maybe records have been lost. Maybe there was a dig years ago. Maybe they got no further than the farm. Sometimes, small sites are just left to nature. There must be hundreds like this, grown over and lost in the landscape."

"You mean like the Gardens of Heligan, waiting to be discovered?"

Simon smiled. "Just like that. Our land is full of the most amazing secrets."

Simon walked with them on the common and Lily told him where everything had been. They showed him the mounds beneath the copse and the spot where the metal detector had leapt with excitement. Lily was impatient while he sought permission to carry out a dig, and she was there, tingling with excitement, when he and his team uncovered the clasps and hinges of a box. The wood itself had gone, but in the soil beneath they found a pair of golden chalices, inlaid with blue lapis lazuli and mother-of-pearl, and a small, beautiful statue of a man with a tiny child on his shoulder.

It was an amazing find. Simon was almost in tears when the treasures were washed and the beauty of the objects was revealed. He hugged Lily and Kate and said that now the evidence had been found there was no way that houses would be built here until a full excavation had been carried out.

The next few weeks were a whirl of activity.

Lily and Kate, Peter and Grandma had special passes that allowed them on the site whenever they pleased. Newspaper reporters came, but Lily's story was not told. Instead, Simon said he had followed a hunch after studying maps and records for years. They all thought it was better that way. And as a thank you, Simon took Kate and Lily to see the remains of the Roman tile factory he had been working on, and then out to lunch.

"I like Simon," said Lily afterwards.

"Me too," said Kate.

****

Chapter 8
New Friends

Of course, the houses didn't get built. The plans were taken elsewhere. Excavations went beneath the remains of the farm to reveal the plan of the priory with its garden and cobbled yard – and one day, when Lily came home from school, Simon took her and her mum and dad on a guided tour. Or rather, Lily took them, telling them where the buttery was and the larder, the dairy and the pastry and the refectory where the nuns ate their meals. She told them about Effie dipping her fingers in the cheese and how they laughed when she was carried out like a sack of potatoes. They walked through the outer gate and across the courtyard. They stood where the orchard had been and Lily smiled, remembering Effie's infectious giggle and cheeky grin – and her bare legs dangling from the apple tree before she jumped.

It was at that very moment that she heard a bark, so familiar that it made her skin tingle, and her stomach turned a somersault.

Kate was startled when she saw the look of astonishment on Lily's face.

"Lupin!" said Lily.

Kate gripped her arm. "No, Lily. It's not Lupin. It's probably the new neighbours. Remember, they're moving in today."

Suddenly, a little dog came through the hedge and bounded towards them. Almost immediately a girl's face appeared above the hedge and a voice called, "Loopy. Come back here, you naughty dog!" Then, "Hello." A hand waved frantically at Lily and Kate, then there was clatter and a rattle and a shriek – and the face disappeared.

Lily and her mum left Simon and ran back towards the gardens with the little dog at their heels. They went through their own garden gate, but before they reached the hedge they shared with their new neighbours, the face suddenly appeared again.

"Sorry! I fell off the boxes. Oh, good! You've got Loopy. He's such a mischief, always getting us both into trouble. He's completely mad. That's why we call him Loopy."

Lily just stared. The twinkle in the girl's green eyes was familiar. So was the cheeky grin.

"I'm Ellie," said the girl, and she held out a grubby hand.

"I'm Lily," said Lily, reaching up.

Their smiles met and even Kate felt the electric tingle in the air that comes when you recognise a friend.

"This is my mum," said Lily.

Kate smiled and lifted the little brown dog over the fence.

"And that's mine," said Ellie, as a lady came into view around the side of the house, "and I'll be in trouble cos I'm supposed to be helping. See you later." And she disappeared.

Then Simon came through the gate – and he was grinning like a schoolboy.

"There's something you haven't seen yet, Lily," he said, and took Lily's hand. "I was keeping it 'til last."

In the remains of the tiny chapel, the archaeologists had uncovered the font, the shallow stone basin by which Effie had made a wish.

Lily ran her fingers around the rim, knowing that Effie had touched it, had dipped her fingers in the holy water.

"Would you like it, Lily?"

Lily nodded slowly, but Kate looked doubtful.

"It's OK, Kate. Everyone's so excited about the other finds they don't mind giving up this one – and we can't leave it on site. It's not like a big Roman dig where there's lots of stonework to put on display in a museum. All we've got left here are the foundations and evidence of later buildings.

"I saw a man shoeing an enormous horse," said Lily.

"They probably had their own smithy," said Simon, and he pulled out some rusty old horseshoe nails from his pocket.

"Can I really have it?" asked Lily, staring at the stone font, and Simon nodded.

"It'll catch the rain," said Kate.

"And the birds can wash in it," added Lily. "Effie would like that, and I don't think the ladies would mind."

Kate looked at Lily's glowing face, happy again after so many weeks.

"Let's have a party," she said.

Ellie and Loopy came, of course. And there was Simon with his son Joshua, and Grandma, Peter and Kate. Afterwards, in the garden, they decided where the new bird bath would go. Lily walked down to the gate in the beech hedge and thought about all she had seen on the other side. Ellie came and stood beside her, warm in the bright red jumper her grandma had made on her knitting machine.

"Last night," said Ellie, "I dreamt there was a wall here, a high stone wall with a big wooden door."

"I've had that dream, too," said Lily.

"I dream silly things," said Joshua, "like I've forgotten to do my homework and instead of Miss Kimble telling me off, she gives me a big box of jelly babies – and they're all green. I hate the green ones."

They all laughed. Then Joshua said. "What's your favourite thing to eat – I mean when you're watching telly or something?"

"Cheese straws," said Lily and Ellie together.

And when they laughed, Loopy jumped up and down and ran circles around them all.

PS. The very next day, the postman brought a letter for Lily. It was from Megan. She'd had chicken pox. She was missing her friend, but school was good and she had made a new friend called Lucy. She hoped Lily liked the red shawl because her grandma said she'd knitted love into it with every stitch. And please would Lily write, even if there was nothing exciting to write about. She just wanted to hear from her friend.

Lily held the letter to her and smiled. Then she put it under her pillow and took out her pencil and paper.

****

In the twelfth century a small priory was founded in North Yorkshire by Roger de Aske for Benedictine nuns. Eight hundred years later a ten-year-old girl sat at the nuns' refectory table enjoying a wonderful farm tea as a guest of the family who then farmed at the old priory. Nibbling the delicious home- made biscuits she looked around her and was fascinated by the stone fireplace set about with carved likenesses of the nuns who once lived there. She was convinced that the six feet thick walls hid passages and tunnels - and kept turning around to check up on the enormous sideboard with feet like lion's paws.

She never forgot that day, and when she read about Isabella Beaufort's escape from the court of Henry the Eighth and about her long, hazardous journey to this tiny Yorkshire priory - dressed as a page, the seeds of a story were sewn.

My thanks to Miss Bainbridge and William for a wonderful tea – and a day that I will never forget.

CPSIA information can be obtained
at www.ICGtesting.com
Printed in the USA
LVHW061815110123
736787LV00012B/76

9 781398 461604